SUPER-AWESOME SCIENCE

THE SCIENCE OF SURVIVAL

by Therese Naber

Content Consultant
Brett C. Woods, PhD
Associate Professor, Department of Biology
University of Wisconsin-Whitewater

Core Library

An Imprint of Abdo Publishing
abdopublishing.com

abdopublishing.com

Published by Abdo Publishing, a division of ABDO, PO Box 398166, Minneapolis, Minnesota 55439. Copyright © 2017 by Abdo Consulting Group, Inc. International copyrights reserved in all countries. No part of this book may be reproduced in any form without written permission from the publisher. Core Library™ is a trademark and logo of Abdo Publishing.

Printed in the United States of America, North Mankato, Minnesota
032016
092016

Cover Photo: Shutterstock Images
Interior Photos: Shutterstock Images, 1; Ryan Rodrick Beiler/Shutterstock Images, 4; Eye of Science/Science Source, 7, 43; Michael & Patricia Fogden/Minden Pictures/Newscom, 10; Red Line Editorial, 12, 30; Christian Musat/Shutterstock Images, 15; iStockphoto, 17, 26; Education Images/UIG/Getty Images, 18; Bill Rome/AlaskaStock/Corbis, 21, 45; Frederique Olivier/Hedgehog House/Minden Pictures/Corbis, 23; Jonathan Mitchell/Atlas Photo Archive/Photoshot/Newscom, 29; Daniel Prudek/iStockphoto, 32; Wes C. Skiles/National Geographic Creative, 34; Everett Kennedy Brown/EPA/Newscom, 37; Fisheye/Mediadrumworld.com/ZumaPress/Newscom, 38; Norbert Wu Minden Pictures/Newscom, 40

Editor: Jon Westmark
Series Designer: Jake Nordby

Publisher's Cataloging in Publication Data
Names: Naber, Therese, author.
Title: The science of survival / by Therese Naber.
Description: Minneapolis, MN : Abdo Publishing, [2017] | Series: Super-awesome science | Includes bibliographical references and index.
Identifiers: LCCN 2015960592 | ISBN 9781680782523 (lib. bdg.) |
    ISBN 9781680776638 (ebook)
Subjects: LCSH: Survival--Juvenile literature
Classification: DDC 613--dc23
LC record available at http://lccn.loc.gov/2015960592

CONTENTS

CHAPTER ONE

FINELY TUNED ANIMALS

The sun blazes over northern Africa's Sahara Desert. The temperature has soared to more than 100 degrees Fahrenheit (38°C). It seems as though nothing could survive in this harsh, sandy landscape.

Then a camel comes into view. It walks slowly down a sand dune. The camel's thick coat insulates its body to keep out heat from the sun. A gust of

Camels' eyes, ears, and nostrils have all adapted to keep sand out.

wind blows sand toward the camel's face. It blinks its long eyelashes and closes its nostrils to keep sand out. The camel has not had water in almost a week, but it is still healthy. This desert wanderer can drink up to 20 gallons (76 L) of water in one session. It uses the water slowly and efficiently. It has been several days since the camel has eaten, but the hump on its back stores fat. The camel's body turns this fat into energy.

Changing to Survive

Camels are one of many species that survive in extreme environments. Tardigrades are creatures

Tardigrades

Tardigrades are tiny animals. They are approximately 0.01 to 0.02 inches (0.25–0.5 mm) long. But these creatures are excellent survivors. In 2007 scientists put thousands of tardigrades on a satellite and launched it into low-Earth orbit. When the satellite landed, many of the tardigrades had survived the trip to space. Tardigrades survive by going into a resting state. Their bodily processes nearly stop. The animal becomes a tun, or dry husk. It can stay like this for decades and become active when it comes into contact with water.

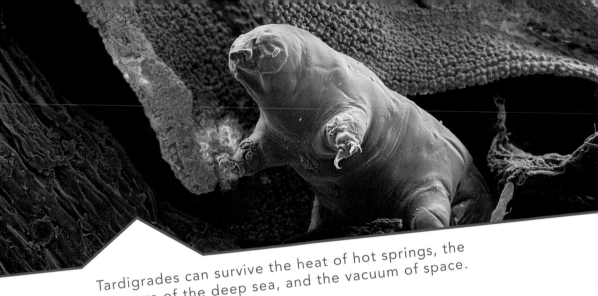

Tardigrades can survive the heat of hot springs, the pressure of the deep sea, and the vacuum of space.

that can live in sea ice. Bar-headed geese migrate over the towering Himalayas of southern Asia. Giant squid survive in the depths of the sea. How do creatures live in these places? Like all living species, they have adapted.

Adaptations are changes in a species over a long time. Traits that help the species survive are passed down from generation to generation. Adaptations can be structural or behavioral. A structural adaptation involves changes in something physical, such as the feathers on a bird or the fur on a bear. A behavioral adaptation is a change in an activity of a population of animals, such as birds migrating to survive winter.

Humans have also developed some natural adaptations for living in challenging conditions. For example, scientists have found physical differences between populations that spend their lives at high altitudes and populations that spend their lives at sea level. But most human adaptations are behavioral. This type of adaptation includes making technologies that allow humans to do things they otherwise would not be able to do. Behavioral adaptations allow humans to survive in some of the most difficult circumstances on Earth and beyond.

IN THE REAL WORLD

The Human Thermostat

The "thermostat" for the human body is located in the brain. Nerves in the skin send temperature information to the brain. If areas are too cold or hot compared to the brain's temperature, messages are sent back to nerves and glands to adjust. Too cold, and a message causes muscles to shiver. This creates heat. Too hot, and a message goes to the sweat glands to start perspiration. When the sweat evaporates, it cools the skin.

The following excerpt is from a book about how humans survive in extreme conditions. The author describes ways humans adapt to different environments:

> Man is the most adaptable of animals. He can live in the tropics, in the Arctic, in deep caves, and on high mountains. With the aid of special equipment he can survive for prolonged periods even in the depths of the sea and in outer space. . . . In extreme environments, behavioral adaptation, including wearing appropriate clothing, is at least as important as physiological adaptation and, in environments unnatural to a terrestrial animal (under water and in outer space), man can survive only with the aid of devices to maintain an immediate environment compatible with human life.

> Source: A. W. Sloan. Man in Extreme Environments. *Springfield, IL: Thomas, 1979. Print. 3.*

Consider Your Audience

Adapt this passage for a different audience, such as your teacher or friends. Write a blog post conveying this same information for the new audience. How does your post differ from the original text and why?

CHAPTER TWO

THE HOTTEST PLACES

The world's hottest climate is found in deserts. The temperature range in deserts is especially extreme because of the lack of cloud cover. Without clouds, the sun's rays go directly to the ground. This makes the ground heat up quickly during the day and cool off quickly at night. Rain helps cool off warm ground, but deserts get little rain. It often occurs in short bursts and evaporates quickly. Because

A bushy tail protects the cape ground squirrel of southern Africa from the sun's harsh rays.

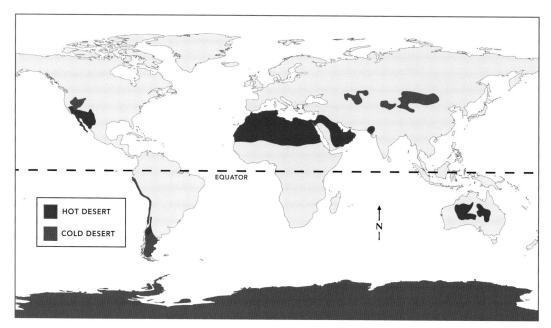

Earth's Deserts

Deserts are areas that receive less than 10 inches (25 cm) of rain per year. Many deserts are hot, but deserts can also be cold. Look at the map of hot and cold deserts. What do you notice about where the hot and cold deserts are located?

of these conditions, plants, animals, and people have had to adapt in different ways to survive.

Desert Plants

Many plants that grow in deserts are succulents. These plants usually have thick, waxy coatings that help them store water. A shallow root system allows them to take in water quickly when it rains. Cacti are one type of succulent.

Succulents have developed ways to protect themselves against animals looking for water. Many cacti have prickly spines for protection. Other succulents are toxic or camouflaged.

All plants need carbon dioxide, sunlight, and water to make food through photosynthesis. Plants have tiny openings called stomata to help with the process. Stomata open in order to take in carbon dioxide. But the openings also let out water. Desert plants cannot afford to lose much water. They have adapted to have fewer stomata per square inch than plants living in other habitats. Many desert plants have also adjusted the time at which they open their stomata. More water will evaporate if a plant opens them during the day. So desert plants open their stomata at night, when it's cooler. This helps them keep water while also getting enough carbon dioxide for photosynthesis.

Animals in the Desert

Most mammals and birds have the internal ability to control their body temperatures. Almost all reptiles do not have this ability. They use the environment to control their body temperatures. This is why lizards in the desert perch on rocks. They are taking in heat from the sun and the rocks. If they get too hot, they might move onto cooler rocks in the shade.

Desert mammals have many physical adaptations. They may have larger ears in relation to body size than animals that live in

Thorny Devil Lizard

The thorny devil lizard is a strange-looking reptile that lives in the Australian desert. Its body is up to eight inches (20 cm) long and covered with spiny thorns. It has a knob behind its head called a false head. When threatened, the lizard tucks its real head between its legs and shows the false head. This protects the animal while making it appear alert. The thorny lizard has a very special way of getting water. Its skin can take in water and move it through tiny grooves to the lizard's mouth.

A fennec fox's ears help it keep cool. They also help the animal listen for bugs to eat.

cooler temperatures. The fennec fox has ears that are six inches (15 cm) tall. That is almost one-quarter of the fox's overall size. Its large ears allow there to be many blood vessels close to the skin. This lets heat from the fox's blood exit the body more easily. Like the camel, the fennec fox has thick fur that helps keep out the sun's heat. And fur on the animal's feet protects the fox from the burning-hot sand. Like other

15

Heat Transfer

Heat transfer is the movement of heat energy between an object and its surroundings. The larger the difference in temperature between the two, the faster heat moves. The size of the objects also affects this rate. Small animals, such as mice, have a large surface area compared to volume. So they lose heat very quickly. They must eat a lot compared to their size to replace lost energy. Large animals, such as elephants, have a small surface area compared to volume. They lose heat much more slowly. An elephant's large ears add surface area to its body. This helps it lose heat faster.

desert mammals, the fox's kidneys have adapted to a lack of water in the desert by limiting water loss.

Mammals in the desert also have behavioral adaptations. Some animals dig into the sand and make dens underground, where it is cooler. Several animals, such as the fennec fox, are nocturnal. This means they are more active at night, when temperatures are cooler. Some animals, such as coyotes and jackrabbits, are more active at twilight.

Loose-fitting clothing billows with movement. This helps cooling air flow over the skin.

Humans in the Heat

Humans also use behavioral adaptations to deal with the heat. Similar to desert animals, we often limit activity during the day. We also often wear several layers of loose-fitting clothing that completely cover the body. Covering so completely might seem odd, but it is actually better. Loose clothing allows for air circulation, which evaporates sweat. The layer also protects from the hot sun.

CHAPTER THREE

THE COLDEST PLACES

As much as one-half of Earth's land is covered with snow and ice for part of the year. Heat flows from warm to cold objects. So all animals that keep their body temperatures higher than their environments' temperatures lose heat constantly. To survive the cold, people and animals have had to adapt. This includes changes to what covers them and how they shelter.

Many people wear animal furs for their insulating abilities.

Fat, Fur, and Feathers

Animals have different kinds of insulation to protect them from cold. Many have thick fur or feathers. These keep animals warm by trapping air near their bodies. Heat does not travel well through air. So keeping air near their bodies helps animals keep from losing heat. For the same reason, humans often wear layers in the cold. The layers trap air. They provide better insulation than wearing one thick layer.

For some animals, fur or feathers give enough insulation for them to live in water. For example, sea otters have dense fur—

Frozen Frogs

Four species of frogs have a special way to survive extreme cold. They do not try to stay warm. Instead they freeze themselves during the winter. They then unfreeze when it warms up. Nearly two-thirds of the water in their bodies freezes. They are able to survive because, even though ice crystals form between cells, the cells do not freeze. The cells are protected by a large amount of sugar. Sugar lowers the temperature at which the cells freeze. This limits the amount of ice that forms in the frog.

Sea otters keep their fur fluffed up to create a layer of air between the cold water and their skin.

up to a million hairs per square inch. This fur traps air and keeps the otter warm. Other animals, such as seals, whales, and polar bears, have thick layers of fat under their skin to stay warm. Unlike muscle and skin, heat does not move easily through fat. The fat keeps animals' warmth in their bodies.

Migration, Hibernation, and Huddling

Animals also have behavioral adaptations to survive in the cold. Some animals leave cold areas. They migrate to warmer places during winter months. Animals that do not migrate might hibernate. This means they spend the winter in a sleeplike state. They use very little energy. Some animals take shelter in holes or under the snow, which insulates against the cold.

Emperor penguins have a unique way of preserving their heat. They huddle together. Groups of thousands gather to stay warm. Antarctic winters can get as cold as −58 degrees Fahrenheit (−50°C), with winds up to 120 miles per hour (200 km/h). Scientists have found that the distance between penguins in the huddle is important. It is best if the birds are touching slightly. If they are too close, this can compress their feathers and make the insulation less effective. Penguins sense this. If one penguin

Adult emperor penguins shield their chicks to keep them warm.

gets too close, the next one moves. A wave of motion travels through the group.

Humans in the Cold

Most human adaptations for surviving in the cold are behavioral. But some research has found that people

Buildings on Stilts

Siberia, in northern Asia, contains some of the coldest places on Earth. Temperatures can drop as low as −76 degrees Fahrenheit (−60°C) in winter. In summer, temperatures can rise to 104 degrees Fahrenheit (40°C). The top layer of soil becomes unstable when it warms up. This layer can be from 3 to 20 feet (1–6 m) deep. Buildings must be built deep into the frozen layer. Otherwise they could crash down. The solution is to build on concrete and steel stilts. These go deep into the frozen layer and keep buildings stable.

living in Arctic regions have a metabolism up to 33 percent higher than people who do not live in cold places. The main explanation for this is that the traditional diet in these areas is high in protein and fat. This type of diet increases metabolism. A higher metabolism creates more body heat.

Humans make shelter with insulation to protect them from the cold. Traditionally in Arctic regions, people have made igloos to do this. An igloo is a shelter made out of blocks of snow. People today use more complex insulated homes.

Traditional Arctic clothing is highly adapted to the environment. Parkas, boots, and pants are made from native animals, such as caribou and musk oxen. The clothing takes advantage of animals' natural insulation. Scientists have studied animal insulation. Insulated clothing has been created using technology from what those studies found.

FURTHER EVIDENCE

Chapter Three discusses animals' adaptations to the cold. The website below also discusses this topic. How is the information from the website the same as the information in Chapter Three? What new information did you learn from the website?

Eight Ways Animals Survive Winter

mycorelibrary.com/science-of-survival

CHAPTER FOUR

THE HIGHEST PLACES

High altitude is defined as 10,000 feet (3,000 m) above sea level. Less than 1 percent of people live at this height. High altitudes are often very cold. But survival there is also challenging because of lower atmospheric pressure. At high altitude, air molecules are farther apart. There is less air pressure as a result. Less pressure makes it more difficult to take oxygen into the lungs. Yet animals, people, and

The Alpine ibex lives in rocky, high-altitude mountains in central Europe, northern Africa, and central Asia.

Timberline

Trees grow in many different conditions. But they cannot grow above certain elevations. This is called the tree line, or the timberline. It is the point where there is not enough warmth, nutrients, or water for trees to live. Strong winds at higher elevation can also damage trees. The tree line may look like a clear line from the distance. But it is actually more gradual. Smaller trees do not need as much food and water. So near the timberline, trees start to get smaller and shorter. At a certain elevation, conditions are too harsh for any trees to survive.

plants manage to survive through adaptations.

Acclimatization

It is possible for people to adjust to high-altitude conditions, but it takes time. Someone coming from low altitude needs to move higher slowly. Even when adjusting slowly, people can develop altitude sickness. This causes headache, nausea, and fatigue. It can even be deadly.

Scientists have found that people who live in high altitudes have developed physical adaptations. The people born in the Andes Mountains of South America are one example. They are generally smaller.

Tibetans have also developed physical adaptations that allow them to work hard at high altitudes.

They also have larger chests with larger lungs. Their hearts pump blood more efficiently as a result. Their blood cells carry oxygen more effectively than those of people living at low altitudes. Their lungs and tissues take up oxygen more efficiently.

Animals at High Altitude

The Himalaya mountain range includes the highest mountains in the world. Yet many animal species live

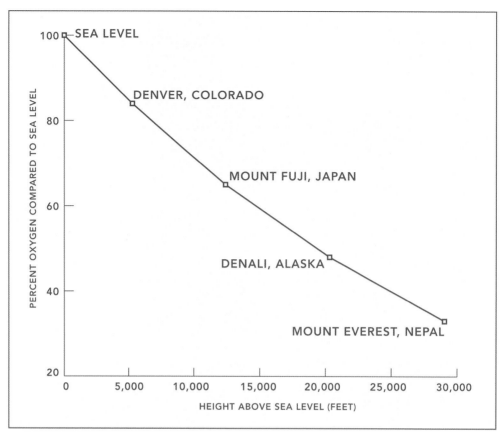

Oxygen and Altitude

This graph shows the amount of oxygen you would breathe in at each height relative to sea level. How does seeing the data laid out in this way help you understand air pressure?

in the mountains, including tigers, monkeys, bears, and more than 340 species of birds. Just like humans, animals have had to adapt to survive at high elevation.

The red panda lives at altitudes from 5,900 to 13,000 feet (1,800–3,900 m). Unlike some animals that move to lower altitudes in winter, the red panda stays high up. Doing so means the animal avoids predators. But it also faces extreme cold and lack of food. Bamboo is the panda's main food source. Red pandas can spend up to 13 hours per day looking for food. In winter, they may lose up to 15 percent of their body weight. Their thick fur helps protect them from the cold. But to survive the cold with little food, red pandas must also slow down their metabolism.

IN THE REAL WORLD

Tigers Up High

In 2010 scientists discovered that tigers in the Himalayas are living at higher altitudes than previously thought. Researchers left camera traps between 9,800 and 13,000 feet (3,000–4,000 m). The scientists checked the cameras three months later. They found a surprising amount of wildlife, including an adult male and adult female Bengal tiger.

The images show that tigers are able to live at higher elevations. All types of tiger subspecies are endangered, with only 3,000 left in the wild. Finding tigers at high elevation is important because it shows a wider range of where they can live. This information could help plans to save the species.

Yaks live in high-altitude areas throughout Asia.

The yak is another high-altitude survivor. It manages to live above 15,700 feet (4,800 m). It has two layers of fur to help it survive the cold. Its heart and lungs are enlarged so it can get enough oxygen. Yaks have adapted so well to high elevation that they need time to adjust to lower elevations. Lower elevations tend to be warmer. Yaks experience heat exhaustion at temperatures above 59 degrees Fahrenheit (15°C).

Andrew Lock is an Australian mountain climber. He has climbed Mount Everest twice. In an excerpt from his book *Master of Thin Air*, he describes acclimating to Everest Base Camp, which is at approximately 17,000 feet (5,181 m):

> *Acclimatizing to the Base Camp altitude simply means you have adjusted enough not to drop dead right then and there. Of course, as you proceed up the mountain you must continue to acclimatize, and even that will allow you only the briefest moment on the summit. It is a long, slow process, taking about a month at 4,000 meters [13,123 feet] or higher to be sufficiently acclimatized to make an attempt on an 8,000-meter [26,246-foot] summit.*

> Source: A. Lock. *Master of Thin Air. New York: Arcade Publishing, 2014. Print. 34.*

What's the Big Idea?

Take a close look at the passage. What is the main point the author makes about the process of getting used to high elevations? How does his description relate to the information about high elevations you read about in Chapter Four?

CHAPTER FIVE

THE DEEPEST PLACES

Oceans cover 71 percent of Earth's surface. They contain 97 percent of the planet's water. They form the largest habitat on Earth. Yet 95 percent of the sea is unexplored. One reason humans have not explored more of Earth's oceans is because doing so is difficult. They are cold, dark, and very deep.

Divers explore a cave on Andros Island, Bahamas.

The Ama Pearl Divers of Japan

For more than 2,000 years, women in Japan, called Ama, have been diving for pearls and shellfish. They can dive up to 98 feet (30 m) deep. They can stay underwater for two minutes at a time. To do this, the divers hyperventilate before diving. They breathe very quickly to lower the amount of carbon dioxide in their bodies. Usually a buildup of carbon dioxide tells a diver's brain the person needs to breathe. Without as much carbon dioxide built up when they dive, the pearl divers can stay underwater for longer without having more oxygen.

Water Pressure

Besides the lack of breathable air, water pressure is the main challenge for humans who hope to spend time in the ocean. Water is much denser and heavier than air. The deeper underwater people go, the more water is stacked on top of them. The pressure increases quickly. For every 33 feet (10 m) of depth, the pressure increases by 14.5 pounds per square inch (1 kg/cm^2). If humans want to go deep, they must breathe in air that is at the same

Divers use breathing techniques to decrease the effect of pressure on their bodies.

pressure as the surrounding water. Otherwise, the pressure surrounding them will crush them.

Humans can use compressed air to survive underwater. Compressed air for divers contains both oxygen and nitrogen. The nitrogen gets dissolved into the blood. It remains there during the dive. To safely move up from deep water, divers need to move slowly because water pressure decreases as they move up

Sperm whales can dive to depths of more than one mile (1.6 km).

toward the surface. If they move too quickly, there is not enough time for the nitrogen to clear from the blood. Instead it separates and forms bubbles in the tissues and blood. This can cause an illness called decompression sickness, also known as the bends.

Sea Animal Adaptations

Some sea mammals' bodies have adapted to avoid getting the bends. Whales and elephant seals dive very deep into the ocean and do not get sick. Their bodies have developed ways to reduce how much nitrogen is dissolved in their tissues. They also breathe out before diving. This reduces how much air they carry. The air sacs in their lungs can even collapse completely. These adaptations allow whales and elephant seals to dive to very high-pressure depths.

The part of the ocean called the deep sea starts below 656 feet (200 m). Sunlight does not reach this depth. Photosynthesis is impossible here. Yet there is still some light. It is created by bioluminescence. This is a chemical reaction in living things that makes light. It is common among fish, jellyfish, crustaceans, and microbes in the deep ocean. But there is the still not much light, so some fish have developed adaptations such as large eyes to see well.

IN THE REAL WORLD

Life in the Dark

Volcanoes on the ocean floor create hot springs known as hydrothermal vents. Scientists discovered these vents in 1977. They spew toxic gases. The water temperature near the vents ranges from nearly freezing to 750 degrees Fahrenheit (398°C). Scientists found more than 300 species living near the vents. More than 95 percent of them were new to science. These organisms use a process called chemosynthesis to change the toxic gases into useable forms of energy.

Anglerfish use bioluminescence to attract prey.

Because photosynthesis cannot happen deep in the ocean, food is usually scarce. A lot of the food at lower depths is the remains of algae, plants, and animals from higher up. As a result, creatures have developed different ways to feed. Gulper eels eat small crustaceans. They have incredibly large mouths to gather as much food as possible.

No matter where a creature lives in the ocean, body color is important. Many animals have camouflage to protect them from predators. The camouflage's color depends on the area in which the animal lives. Some animals, such as jellyfish and some squid, are even transparent. This makes them difficult to see in open water.

All species on Earth each have many adaptations. Some seem more extreme to us. But all living things are specialized in the art of survival.

EXPLORE ONLINE

James Cameron is a famous filmmaker. He is also an enthusiastic deep-sea explorer. On March 26, 2012, he made a record-breaking solo dive to the deepest place on Earth. He dove down nearly seven miles (11 km) into the Mariana Trench off the coast of Guam. Look at the expedition's website. What are the challenges of underwater exploration discussed in this chapter? How did the expedition deal with these challenges?

Deep-Sea Challenge

mycorelibrary.com/science-of-survival

FAST FACTS

- Adaptations are changes that help a species survive. A behavioral adaptation is a change in an activity. A structural adaption involves physical changes to the species.
- Heat transfer is the movement of heat energy between an object and its surroundings. The larger the difference in temperature between the two, the faster heat energy is transferred. Surface area and volume of the object also affect this rate.
- Some animals use fur or feathers to trap air next to their bodies. This helps insulate their bodies from the cold. Other animals use thick layers of fat for insulation. Heat does not travel easily through fat.
- Air molecules are farther apart at high altitude. This makes it more difficult to take in oxygen.

- Water pressure increases with depth. For every 33 feet (10 m) of depth, the pressure increases by 14.5 pounds per square inch (1 kg/cm²).

Tell the Tale

Chapter One describes a camel in the desert. Imagine you are traveling with the camel in the desert. Write 200 words about your trip. What plants and animals do you see? What do you do during the day? What do you do at night? What do you need to do to survive?

Why Do I Care?

Maybe you do not live in a place with extreme conditions. That does not mean you cannot think about some of the adaptations necessary to survive. What adaptations do you see in people or animals in your own environment? Are they physical or behavioral?

Say What?

Studying extreme environments can involve a lot of new vocabulary terms. Find five words in this book you've never heard before. Use a dictionary to find out what they mean. Write the meanings in your own words, and use each word in a new sentence.

You Are There

Chapter Five discusses survival in the deep ocean. Imagine you have the opportunity to travel deep into the ocean. Write a letter telling friends about the experience. What did you see? What kinds of plants and animals were there? How did you feel when you were deep in the ocean?

GLOSSARY

camouflage
color or shape that makes something blend into the area around it

chemosynthesis
the process of making food from chemical energy

evaporate
to change from liquid to gas

hibernate
to spend part or all of winter in a dormant state

hydrothermal vent
an opening on the ocean floor where superheated, mineral-rich water comes out

metabolism
chemical reactions in cells that convert food into energy

migrate
to move from one region or habitat to another

photosynthesis
the process in which plants use water, carbon dioxide, and sunlight to make food

succulent
a kind of plant with thick, heavy leaves or stems that store water

LEARN MORE

Books

Chinery, Michael. *Animal Kingdom: Life in the Wild.* London: Lorenz Books, 2011.

Chinery, Michael. *Survival: Amazing Wild Animals in the Natural World.* London: Lorenz Books, 2005.

Zappa, Marcia. *Thorny Devils.* Minneapolis, MN: Abdo Publishing, 2016.

Websites

To learn more about Super-Awesome Science, visit **booklinks.abdopublishing.com**. These links are routinely monitored and updated to provide the most current information available.

Visit **mycorelibrary.com** for free additional tools for teachers and students.

INDEX

ABOUT THE AUTHOR

Therese Naber is a writer who lives in Minnesota. She has written many textbooks for students of English as a second language. This is her fourth nonfiction book for young people.